The Kill Code

2025

Copyright © 2025 Ian McEwan

All rights reserved.

No part of this publication may be reproduced, distributed, or transmitted in any form or by any means, including photocopying, recording, or other electronic or mechanical methods, without the prior written permission of the author, except in the case of brief quotations used in reviews or critical articles.

This is a work of fiction. Names, characters, places, and incidents are either products of the author's imagination or used fictitiously. Any resemblance to actual persons, living or dead, or actual events is purely coincidental.

For permissions or inquiries, please contact:

Chameleon.15026052@gmail.com

www.chameleon-news.com

Contents

Chapter 1 – The Kill Code

Chapter 2 - The Disruptor

Chapter 3 – Cracks in the Armour

Chapter 4 – A Target on His Back

Chapter 5 – The Walls Begin to Crack

Chapter 6 – The Unthinkable Order

Chapter 7 – The Weight of Defiance

Chapter 8 – The Ghosts She Carries

Chapter 9 – The Woman She Became

Chapter 10 – The Unfinished Order

Chapter 11 – The Woman's War

Chapter 12 – The Order Strikes Back

Chapter 15 – The Fracture

Chapter 16 – The Decryption

Chapter 17 - The Hunt for Him

Chapter 18 - Running Together

Chapter 19 - The Insider

Chapter 20 - The Ally's Last Words

Chapter 21 - The Final Test

Chapter 22 - Unravelling the Order

Chapter 24 - Running Through Fire

Chapter 25 - Into the Shadows

Chapter 26 – The Final Trap

Chapter 27 – The Price of War

Chapter 28 – The Counter Move

Chapter 29 – The Ultimatum

Chapter 30 – The Order's Real Game

Chapter 31 – Turning the Trap

Chapter 32 – The Order's Last Move

Chater 33 – Infiltrating the Heart of the Order

Chapter 35 – The Temptation of Power

Chapter 36 - The Final Test

Chapter 37 - Rejecting the Order

Chapter 38 - Erasing the Order

Chapter 39 - The Ghosts That Never Die

Chapter 1 – The Kill Code

The shot was clean. Precise.

A .45-caliber round slipped through the neon haze, slicing into soft tissue just below the executive's left eye. No exit wound. No spray. Just silence.

The body sagged forward at the rooftop table. A glass of overpriced whiskey slid from lifeless fingers, shattering like brittle ice on tile.

No one in the dining area below heard a thing. The suppressor made sure of that.

And if anyone noticed their CEO slumping mid-toast?

They'd take five seconds to react. Five seconds was a lifetime.

The hitman exhaled—slow, deliberate—and slid back from his sniper's nest. His heart rate never spiked. His breath stayed level. His hands moved by instinct, breaking down the rifle, wiping it clean, erasing every trace with practiced grace.

In twenty minutes, police drones would sweep the sector. In thirty, corporate lockdown would seal the zone.

In forty-five?

He'd be gone.

He disappeared into the underbelly of the city—down steel ladders and neon-slick alleys where artificial rain bled into oil puddles. Shadows swallowed his steps.

Just another ghost in a city built to forget men like him.

Everywhere, screens flickered—looped propaganda, toothy smiles, polished lies.

Order is peace. Compliance is purpose.

Obedience is freedom.

The corporations owned the law. The law owned the people.

And the people learned to obey.

When they didn't? The Order stepped in.

Silent. Surgical. Unseen.

Surveillance drones drifted overhead, scanning bios and behaviour. He passed beneath them unnoticed—his genetic profile scrubbed, his presence calibrated to register as unremarkable. That was the point.

The couple who raised him weren't parents. They were engineers.

No lullabies. No warmth. Just doctrine. How to hear a lie before it's spoken.

How to kill without hesitation.

How to vanish before the body hits the floor.

While other children learned math, he mastered penthouse infiltration and mid-sleep executions.

They weren't cruel. Just efficient. Or so they trained him to believe.

Efficiency didn't require love.

And for most of his life, that had been enough. Until now.

He knew how to pass—how to smile at the right moment, say just enough to slip through the cracks.

But he never understood people.

Small talk? Pointless.

Casual relationships? Vulnerabilities. Flirting? A code with no key.

Women were an equation with too many variables. He could read them like targets—micro-expressions, emotional cadence—but he couldn't connect.

And for most of his life, he hadn't cared. Until now.

As a boy, he used to watch the other children laugh—loud, chaotic, free—and wonder what they understood that he didn't.

That memory never lasted. He always buried it.

But now, it surfaced. And this time, it stayed.

At his safehouse, he stripped off gloves, boots, jacket. Routine. Ritual.

He cleaned everything.

The job was done. One more name erased. One more mission sealed in silence.

Then the terminal blinked. An encrypted message.

Not from his handler. Not from the usual relay.

Off-grid.

That wasn't protocol.

He decrypted the message.

EXECUTION VERIFIED. PHASE ONE COMPLETE.

STAND BY FOR NEXT INSTRUCTIONS. DO NOT ATTEMPT TO LOCATE US.

For the first time in years, his pulse caught. Stumbled.

This wasn't just a contract. This was something else.

Something larger. Unclear.

Or maybe the kill was never the point.

Maybe he was part of a larger test—one he never agreed to take.

He stared at the screen as unease moved down his spine, cold and mechanical.

This message hadn't come from anyone he knew. And for the first time, he wasn't sure who had pulled the trigger.

Had it ever been the same people? Had he ever known?

His exit instructions were clear: burn the safehouse, erase the trail, disappear.

Standard protocol. But now?

He wasn't going anywhere. Not yet.

Because the only way to win against people playing a deeper game... Was to pretend he hadn't noticed the board.

He needed intel.

And intel meant leverage.

Leverage meant someone who had access to channels he wasn't supposed to know existed.

So, he did something he never did. He stepped into the open.

The Neon District — 02:30 Hours

The club was loud. Dense with sweat, smoke, and delusion. Bodies packed together under shifting light. People pretending to matter.

Elites. Syndicate muscle. Corporate suits with surgically curated faces.

He hated places like this. Too much motion. Too many eyes.

But she would be here.

She owed him. Even if she'd never admit it.

She sat where he expected—corner booth, crimson dress, eyes scanning the crowd even as she feigned boredom.

Not trust. Not friendship. Just history.

Mara Li. Fixer. Broker. The kind of woman who could smell a lie before it left your lips—and knew when to treat a killer like a consultant.

She looked up as he slid into the booth. Her grip on her glass tightened. Something sharp and expensive.

"I heard about your little rooftop performance," she said. Smooth. Testing.

He didn't flinch. "I need answers."

"And I need early retirement." A shrug. "We all have dreams."

He leaned forward. "Who else was on the contract?" She paused.

Only a second.

But that was enough.

Mara didn't hesitate. Unless she was afraid.

She leaned in, voice low. "You should walk away from this one."

"I don't walk."

She sighed. Set the glass down. "Then I hope you enjoy ghosts."

He didn't blink. "Tell me."

Her eyes flicked. Not if she should answer—how much she could say without dying.

"It wasn't your usual network," she said. "Someone higher. Off-map. Even the Order pretends they don't exist." And then—he felt it.

Not from Mara. From the room.

A pressure. Stillness.

Too many people, too quiet.

He spotted the glint—pistol at the bar, angled just so. Trained. Professional.

Not here to talk.

Mara's voice cut the air: "Damn it. You led them here—" Too late.

The first shot missed. The second didn't.

He flipped the table, dragging Mara down as the booth exploded in a hail of gunfire.

Screams. Chaos. Bodies clawing for exits.

This wasn't a warning. This was a purge.

He drew his sidearm, firing blind, moving faster than panic could catch up.

Seconds. Maybe less.

Mara grabbed his wrist as he pulled her toward the exit.

"You want answers?" Her voice sharp. Urgent. "Then stop looking for names."

She shoved something into his hand.

A data chip. No bigger than a thumbnail.

"This is bigger than you. Bigger than the Order. You weren't supposed to see it. The list. The real one. This wasn't just a hit—it was Phase One."

She pushed him back.

He turned. "You won't walk out of this."

She smiled.

That kind of smile—the one that knows the odds and stands anyway.

"Then make it mean something." Gunfire swallowed her words.

He ran.

Outside, the shadows took him. A ghost again.

His pulse? Steady. His hands? Still.

But his mind?

Fracturing.

The encrypted message. The kill team.

The second layer of the contract.

The Order didn't just want him dead. They wanted him erased.

He turned the chip over in his palm. Still warm.

Mara died for this. Now he had a choice:

Disappear forever... Or go deeper.

And the worst part?

He already knew his answer.

Chapter 2 - The Disruptor

The lounge pulsed with a slow, deliberate rhythm— a heartbeat for the city's underworld.

Smoke curled through low-lit air.

Neon reflections slid across crystalline glasses filled with overpriced liquor.

The people here weren't just rich. They were untouchable.

Crime lords. Corporate brokers. Black-market fixers. Deals whispered in corners. Fortunes shattered with a glance.

The hitman didn't belong here. And yet, he belonged everywhere.

Seated in the farthest corner, he was just another ghost among kings.

He wasn't here to drink. He was here to watch.

To the right people, his presence meant something. A contract was coming.

Another name. Another life erased.

The job always came first.

His handler had sent him to wait. Passive assignment. Low risk.

But waiting was its own kind of skill.

The Order didn't always need a trigger pulled. Sometimes they needed silence.

And someone like him to hold it.

Patience kept you alive. Impulse got you killed.

He stayed still.

Watching.

Who was dangerous. Who was pretending.

Who was waiting for someone like him to move first.

And then— Someone did.

She moved like she wasn't afraid. Not hesitant. Not cautious.

Deliberate.

She slid into the seat across from him, setting down her glass with a kind of ease that said she'd done this before.

Most people avoided him without knowing why. She did the opposite.

She'd studied men like this. Cold. Purpose-built.

But something about him didn't fit the pattern. (Even if he didn't see it yet.)

He didn't react. Didn't acknowledge her. Let the silence stretch.

Most people broke under it. She didn't.

She smiled—slow and knowing. Like she'd already solved him,

and was waiting for him to catch up.

"You've been watching them all night," she said, nodding toward the room.

"But nobody's watching you." He said nothing.

Silence was a weapon. And he wielded it well.

She didn't flinch. Didn't retreat.

Instead, she leaned in. Not like a flirt—like a scientist studying something rare. "Is that your trick?" she asked.

"Stay so quiet people forget you're there?" He met her eyes. Scanning.

Women didn't talk to him without motive. But she wasn't nervous.

Wasn't afraid.

And that unsettled him more than a threat would have.

"You don't belong here," she said. Soft. More to herself.

"Neither do you."

His voice was flat. Uninviting.

She smiled like it was a compliment.

And for the first time in a very long time, he didn't feel like a weapon.

He felt... seen.

The sensation hit too fast to define. Too deep to ignore.

Women had approached him before— For power. For money. For leverage.

This was different.

She wasn't seeking. She was observing.

Most people filled silence with noise. She let it breathe.

"You don't talk much," she noted. "Or you don't like talking."

"I don't waste words." "Efficient."

He didn't respond.

She smirked.

"Terrible with people, though."

That landed.

He didn't know why.

It wasn't pity.

It wasn't mockery. It was just true.

Something uncoiled in his chest. Low. Tight.

A knot he hadn't realized was there.

"Do you even know how to flirt?" she asked, teasing. He didn't blink.

"Not useful."

She laughed.

Not coy.

Not calculated.

Just real.

And for some reason, it twisted in his gut. "That's the most practical thing I've ever heard." He looked away—just for a second.

Not embarrassment. Not attraction.

Something else.

He didn't like it. But he didn't leave.

There was no strategic reason to stay. No intel. No leverage. No mission.

And yet— he stayed.

Not because he wanted something. Not because she posed a threat.

But because she wasn't afraid of him.

And stranger still...a part of him didn't want her to be.

She finished her drink, stood smoothly, and looked down at him.

"See you around, ghost." He watched her go.

Unease rising.

Something about her didn't fit. He was good at patterns.

Good at spotting threats.

And yet—he didn't know what she was.

But for the first time... he wanted to find out.

Chapter 3 – Cracks in the Armour

He shouldn't be thinking about her.

Yet as he moved through the city's underbelly—neon-lit alleys, dead-eyed pedestrians, rain slicking off steel—her voice echoed in his mind.

"See you around, ghost."

It was irrelevant. She was irrelevant.

And yet... she lingered.

That didn't happen. He didn't let things linger.

But the way she looked at him—unafraid, amused, like he

was a puzzle instead of a threat—stuck in his mind like shrapnel.

His thoughts moved like gears: threats, opportunities, efficiency.

She was none of those things.

So why the hell was she still there?

He'd been trained to discard moments like that. But this one kept surfacing—

like a glitch in his programming.

The encrypted message came through at midnight. New name. New target.

Standard protocol.

But this one was different.

The intel was sparse. The dossier lacked depth. The target's defences were military-grade—layered, shielded, calculated.

This wasn't a job. It was a test.

And still...That last message echoed:

EXECUTION VERIFIED. PHASE ONE COMPLETE.

STAND BY FOR NEXT INSTRUCTIONS.

Something was off.

He just didn't know what.

He used to follow orders without hesitation. Now, every directive came with an echo:

Why?

Who benefits?

Whose game am I in?

The bar wasn't his kind of place. Too much noise. Too many eyes.

But the intel drop had been set here. Simple pick-up. No contact.

At least, that was the plan.

And then— she appeared.

Like she'd been waiting for him.

She caught his eye across the room and raised her glass in a silent toast.

A normal man would've looked away. Pretended not to notice.

He didn't.

He let her come to him.

"Twice in one week," she said, sliding into the seat across from him.

"I'm starting to think you live in the shadows." He didn't reply.

"Still not much of a talker, huh?"

She smirked. Studying him. Reading him. And he hated how it made him feel.

"You don't do casual conversation, do you?" "No."

She chuckled. "And yet, here you are."

He told himself it was coincidence. That her presence meant nothing.

But his body didn't move.

He could have left. Should have.

But he stayed.

Not because he wanted to.

He didn't know what wanting felt like.

She wasn't impressed. She wasn't intimidated.

She was playing.

And somehow... that made him stay.

"Buy you a drink?" she asked, voice casual.

He hesitated.

Just long enough for her to catch it.

She leaned forward, voice lowering, just enough to feel like a secret.

"Relax, ghost. I'm not trying to sleep with you. Just want to see if you can hold a conversation without malfunctioning."

He should've walked away.

Instead, he said, "One drink."

She talked more. That was fine. He listened.

Watched the rhythm of her speech.

The way her fingers moved when she made a point. The way she tested him—gently, but deliberately.

She wasn't flirting. She was analysing.

Just like him.

"You're profiling me, aren't you?" she asked. He blinked.

No one had ever said that aloud before.

"That's what you do," she smirked.

"You break people down. Study their weaknesses."

He didn't answer. Didn't need to.

She sipped her drink, her eyes never leaving his. "Must be exhausting, living like that."

He hadn't thought about it. It was just the job.

But lately, the job had started leaking into everything. "I wasn't taught how to be normal."

The words escaped before he could stop them.

She didn't flinch.

She just went still. Measured. "Taught?"

He said nothing.

She didn't push.

She just nodded—like she understood more than he wanted her to.

And strangely...that didn't bother him.

What did concern him

was how easy it had been to say it.

Like part of him had been waiting for someone to ask.

The conversation lasted longer than it should've. Time wasted.

Time he wasn't supposed to waste.

When he finally stood to leave— he felt it.

A presence.

Subtle.

Wrong.

Someone was watching him.

He had spent his life being the one who tracked. Now, someone was tracking him.

He didn't react.

He moved toward the exit with precision. Casual. Controlled.

He didn't look over his shoulder. Didn't let them know he knew.

But he felt it.

A shadow in the crowd. Eyes that didn't blink.

Someone was out there.

Maybe linked to his last job. Maybe tied to the message.

Or maybe...The Order hadn't let go of him after all.

Chapter 4 – A Target on His Back

The city was always alive at night. But tonight, it felt different.

He moved through the underbelly's narrow corridors— neon-lit, shadow-soaked, pulsing with static.

His footsteps were silent. His senses, razor-sharp.

Something was wrong. Not paranoia.

Paranoia was fear without cause. This was experience.

Someone was watching.

Not just tracking him—hunting him.

He'd spent a lifetime as a ghost. Unseen. Unnoticed. Untraceable.

But now?

Now, someone had marked him.

He pulled on his network—informants, coded drops, encrypted whispers scattered across the dark web's underbelly.

Only one thing came back:

Nothing.

And nothing didn't happen.

Silence like that meant power. The kind that bought fear.

The kind that made people forget your name. That narrowed it down to the worst of them.

His safehouse was a windowless, forgotten room in a block no one remembered.

No lights. No record.

No reason anyone should know it existed. And yet—

They were waiting.

The moment he opened the door, a shot whispered past his head.

He moved before thought caught up. Training took over.

Automatic fire shredded the doorway behind him, splintering wood and steel.

They weren't amateurs. They were mercenaries.

The high-dollar kind.

He dropped low, ducked into cover. Counted footsteps.

Three.

No—

Four.

They expected him to run. He didn't.

He hunted.

The first died before the knife touched air.

The second turned too late. One shot. Temple. Gone.

The third fired in panic. Mistake.

Dead.

The fourth?

Smart.

He threw a flash grenade.

The room bloomed white.

When the haze cleared—the last mercenary was gone. But he'd left something behind.

Carved into the wall, etched deep with a combat blade:

YOU WERE NEVER MEANT TO SEE IT.

The encrypted message.

The glitch in the contract.

This wasn't about a target anymore. It was about him.

About what he wasn't supposed to know.

Whoever hired the kill squad wasn't just covering tracks. They were sending a message.

And only one organization delivered messages like that.

Not the radicals.

Not the corporations.

The Order.

They didn't issue warnings. They issued consequences.

Someone wanted him to know he was being watched. That they weren't afraid of him.

Which meant—they didn't understand what he was.

He touched his side. Blood. Warm. Superficial.

Still—enough to make him pause. That's when he saw her.

The woman.

Leaning against a rusted railing at the end of the alley, like she'd been waiting for the world to catch up.

"Rough night?" she asked.

His gun was in his hand before she finished speaking. She didn't flinch.

"If you wanted me dead," he said, voice flat, "this is a bad time to try."

She shrugged.

"If I wanted you dead, I'd have let them finish the job." She wasn't wrong.

And that was what bothered him. He didn't trust coincidence.

She'd been there when the encrypted message arrived. She'd been there when doubt crept in.

And now—here she was, after the ambush.

"How did you know?" he asked.

She tilted her head. "I hear things."

He stepped closer. Too close.

"Who do you work for?"

"I could ask you the same thing."

His grip tightened.

Her posture didn't change.

"I'm bleeding," he said. "And you're testing my patience." She sighed.

"You want to keep running blind, be my guest. But if you want answers, you're going to need help."

He studied her.

Every part of him said to walk. She was a variable.

A risk.

A problem.

But then—He thought about the mercenaries.

The message.

The blade-etched warning.

Someone out there wanted him dead—but only after they made sure he understood why. He'd always known what he was:

A ghost.

A tool.

A weapon the Order wielded without question.

But now—standing here, bleeding in the dark, with this woman watching him and not running... He didn't feel like any of those things.

He didn't know what part of him was choosing to stay. But it didn't feel like instinct.

It felt like doubt. And that was new.

"You want to help me?" he asked at last.

She smirked.

"I want to know who you really are." That was the price.

Not protection.

Not loyalty.

Answers.

She was playing her own game.

And against his better judgment— he was going to let her.

For now.

Because whoever had just put a target on his back... Was about to find out what it felt like to be hunted.

Somewhere across the city, in a tower of glass and static, a phone buzzed.

A single message:

He survived.

A pause.

Then the reply:

Of course he did. That was the point.

Chapter 5 – The Walls Begin to Crack

The city was a machine—unforgiving, efficient, built to consume.

He and the woman moved through its veins, slipping down service tunnels and neon-lit alleyways.

Every step was calculated. No wasted motion.

No second chances.

The mercenaries were precise. But he was better.

When he took out the lead operative, the others lost their edge.

The city was his hunting ground. And now?

He was vanishing into it.

But for the first time, he wasn't alone.

And that gnawed at him more than the men trying to kill him.

His safehouses were burned.

The streets—once neutral ground—were hostile now. Someone had mapped him.

Watched him long before he realized it.

This wasn't just an attack. It was a slow suffocation.

A methodical effort to flush him out.

And still—she was there.

That was the part that didn't make sense.

He should've left her behind. Cut her loose.

Forgotten her name.

Instead,he kept her close.

And he didn't know why.

She moved beside him like she belonged. Like she'd been built for this.

Most people would've panicked. Slowed him down with questions.

Not her.

She was calm.

Controlled.

Watching him as carefully as he watched her.

The silence between them wasn't cold. Wasn't empty.

And for the first time, he didn't want it to end.

That was new. And dangerous.

They found shelter in a forgotten high-rise— its walls hollowed by time, its windows fractured into jagged reflections of the skyline.

He leaned against cracked concrete, rolling his shoulder. Pain flared.

The gash along his ribs was deeper than he'd thought. He had no time for wounds.

But she was already in front of him, kneeling with a stolen med kit.

"Let me."

He didn't argue.

She pressed a damp cloth to the wound. He flinched.

Not from pain. From the touch.

And that was worse.

Pain could be processed. Filed away as data.

But this?

This was different.

She wasn't patching him up for a mission. Not to secure an asset. Not to fulfil a contract. She was just... helping.

And he didn't know what to do with that.

She noticed. Of course she did. But she didn't say anything.

And somehow, that made it harder.

The bleeding stopped. The silence stretched.

He was the one who broke it. "Why are you here?"

She smirked.

"Here as in this crumbling building? Or here as in... running

for my life next to you?" "Either."

She tilted her head.

A flicker passed across her face— tight, fleeting, gone.

"That's a lot of curiosity from someone who doesn't ask questions."

He waited.

She sighed, leaning back against the wall. Her voice quieter now.

"Let's just say I have unfinished business. And right now, that means sticking with you."

It wasn't an answer. Not a real one.

A half-truth dressed in sarcasm. He should've pressed her.

Should've peeled it apart.

But he didn't.

Because for once,

he didn't want to dissect someone to understand them. He just wanted to sit in the silence.

And that?

That was more dangerous than the men hunting him. He wasn't used to this.

The stillness.

The space between words.

The way she filled it without intruding.

His life had always been precision. Target. Execute. Disappear.

But this?

This had no blueprint.

She must've seen the shift in him, because she smiled— not with amusement,

but understanding.

"You don't have to know what to say," she said softly. Then, after a beat:

"Just don't shut me out."

The words hit harder than they should have. Because no one had ever said them to him before.

And for the first time, he wondered if he could change. A low ping broke the moment.

Encrypted.

Untraceable.

He turned, pulling the terminal from his jacket. Fingers moved on reflex.

New contract.

New name.

A kill order.

His pulse slowed. His eyes narrowed.

She watched him. Carefully.

"What?" she asked. He hesitated.

For the first time in a long time, he didn't want to answer.

But hiding it would be worse.

So, he turned the screen. Let her see.

The name on the hit list?

Hers.

Chapter 6 – The Unthinkable Order

The screen glowed cold blue.

Her name stared back at him like a loaded gun.

Her name.

He'd killed for less. Much less.

His breath stayed even. His pulse, steady.

His training screamed: Emotion has no place in the equation.

A target is a target.

But this time—logic fractured.

He forced himself to analyse. Rational. Detached.

Why her?

She wasn't powerful.

Not corporate. Not syndicate. Not political. Not officially.

But maybe that was the problem. Maybe she knew something.

Maybe she always had.

His finger hovered over the confirmation key. One tap.

One press.

And she would vanish like all the rest.

His mind ordered him to act.

His instincts whispered it was already too late.

And hesitation? That was death.

She was speaking.

But her voice blurred beneath the roar in his head.

Focus. Breathe. Finish the job.

"You're shutting down again."

His head snapped up. She was watching him. Close.

Too close.

"What happened?"

He said nothing.

Because saying it would make it real. The rules had always been simple:

Never ask why. Never hesitate.

Never let emotion cloud the mission. That's what they drilled into him.

Relentlessly.

The couple who raised him— not parents, just engineers— hadn't raised a son.

They built a tool.

A tool meant to follow. To execute.

To obey.

And now, standing here, with her looking at him like he was something more... He felt the fracture widen.

It had never been loyalty.

It had always been fear.

Fear of doubt. Fear of questions.

Fear of becoming something he didn't know how to be.

She kept talking. Soft. Unaware.

Unprotected.

If she knew what he was thinking, she didn't show it.

His finger twitched.

Still hovering above her name.

He wanted to do it. God help him—he wanted the clarity.

The comfort of obedience. The silence.

But the silence didn't feel safe anymore. It felt like a trap.

Then she did something simple. She smiled.

Not to manipulate. Not to seduce.

Not to disarm.

Just... because he was there.

And in that moment—he knew.

He couldn't do it.

His thumb moved. Not to confirm.

To delete.

The contract vanished. Gone.

No alarms.

No override.

No second message demanding compliance. Just silence.

The kind that comes before a clean-up crew. He stared at the empty screen.

Expecting resolution. Expecting relief.

But it didn't feel like mercy. It felt like mutiny.

Somewhere— on some server,

in some command centre—a flag had already been raised.

One refusal.

One deviation.

And the countdown had begun.

Whoever had sent the order— whoever had been watching—

They would know.

And in their eyes, he had just crossed the line.

From asset... to threat.

He didn't tell her what he'd done. He couldn't.

But he did something else. Something even more dangerous.

He asked her to stay close. Not to protect her.

Not even to protect himself. But because right now—she was the only thing anchoring him to something human.

Chapter 7 – The Weight of Defiance

The hitman sat in the dim glow of the safehouse, the only light coming from his encrypted device.

The contract was gone.

Deleted.

But nothing happened.

No override.

No retaliation.

No second message demanding compliance. Just silence.

And for the first time in his life, that silence felt wrong.

Not because of guilt. He didn't feel guilt.

But because his entire existence had been built on obedience.

And now, for the first time, he had broken the code.

His eyes drifted to the data chip on the table— still smudged with a faint streak of Mara's blood.

He hadn't cleaned it.

Couldn't.

Her final words echoed, sharp and unfinished.

"You weren't supposed to see it."

Whatever it was, she had died for it.

And that meant something.

Someone had marked him— not just as an asset, but as a threat.

If she died for this, then there had to be a reason.

And if it involved him, he was already compromised.

His "family"—or whatever they had been— had controlled everything.

Contracts.

Purpose.

Identity.

A target arrived. He executed.

He vanished.

That was the rhythm.

The only rhythm he had ever known.

No face.

No name.

No voice behind the orders.

Only encrypted signals. Anonymous deposits.

Unquestioned expectations.

And until now, he'd never questioned any of it. Because it never mattered.

But now?

Now it did.

Because the moment he chose not to follow the order, he realized something:

He had no idea who had ever been giving them.

And that—that unsettled him more than anything.

She watched him the way he once watched targets— reading posture, measuring tension.

She saw the tightness in his shoulders. The way his eyes lingered near doorways.

The breath he didn't realize he was holding.

She tried to break it. A joke.

A smile.

A tease.

He didn't respond.

"What happened?" she asked. He didn't speak.

Because saying it aloud would make it real.

And real things had consequences. The silence stretched.

Maybe the system was slow.

Maybe the breach hadn't registered. Maybe—No.

They always knew. Hours passed.

Still nothing.

And that's when the paranoia set in.

Outside, the city changed.

Subtly. Deliberately.

Drones lingered longer near windows. Their scan patterns were just… off.

Figures moved in alleys. Never close.

Never fast.

But present.

Watching.

He checked every line. Every loop.

Every backdoor.

Nothing.

And that was worse than an execution order.

Because this wasn't silence. It was strategy.

They weren't reacting. They were waiting.

Flashes of his past returned.

Not memories— instructions.

The voice of his earliest mentor, sharp as a blade: "You are a tool. Nothing more, nothing less."

He remembered the taste of metal— from training.

From punishment.

From the days he was still learning to suppress his questions.

He had been trained not to hesitate. Not to think.

Not to wonder. But now?

Now he was still breathing.

And that raised a deeper question: If they still saw him as just an asset... why wasn't he already dead?

She leaned against the cracked window, watching the neon skyline blink in silence.

Unaware.

Unprepared.

She didn't know it yet.

He didn't fully know it yet. But this wasn't silence.

It was recalibration.

They were watching. Waiting.

Measuring deviation.

And when they finally moved?

There would be no message. No warning.

Just a breath in the dark—and then the world would burn.

Chapter 8 – The Ghosts She Carries

The room was quiet, save for the hum of the city bleeding through cracked windows.

Neon flickered across the broken glass, casting fractured light over concrete and silence.

He sat at the far end of the safehouse, posture loose, calm.

But she knew better. His body was still.

His mind wasn't.

He thought she didn't notice. But she always noticed.

She watched him the way he watched threats— precisely, patiently, like a puzzle that shouldn't exist.

And she knew something was coming.

Not because of instinct. Not because of fear.

Because it always did.

She had lived this moment before—the breath before a truth breaks everything.

She was never just a woman in a bar. Never just curious.

Never just there.

She had a reason. A mission.

Years spent chasing ghosts— decoding encrypted ruins, cutting through lies

woven by a system built to erase people like her. And somehow, all of it had led her to him.

A man who thought himself untethered, a ghost without a past, without a future.

But he wasn't the only one haunted.

She hadn't been raised to kill.

She wasn't moulded in steel and silence. She was raised in a lie.

Her family had belonged to something larger— a resistance,

a rebellion, a war the world had no record of.

They fought the same machine that shaped him.

The same invisible regime

hiding behind laws, logos, and Order. And they lost.

She remembered the night it ended. The gunfire.

The broken door. The final silence.

She was too young to fight. Too young to stop it.

But not too young to understand. Not too young to carry the weight.

And she had.

For years.

It wasn't fate.

It wasn't coincidence.

She hadn't found him by accident. She had hunted him.

Because she knew what he was. What made him.

Who controlled him.

The faceless handlers behind encrypted directives— the architects of precision death—they were the same ones who destroyed her family.

And now…she was close.

Closer than she'd ever been. Close to understanding.

Close to the truth. Close to him.

Too close.

She had come into his life with a plan.

He was a means. A key.

A weapon she could redirect.

Just another killer, built by the enemy.

But then— she saw it.

The cracks.

The hesitation.

The way he looked at her— not like a mission asset, but like she was something he couldn't define.

He wasn't just a machine. He wasn't clean.

He was unravelling.

And in that unravelling— he reminded her of herself.

Lost.

Alone.

Built for something she no longer believed in.

And that?

That was dangerous.

Because it made her want things she couldn't afford.

Trust.

Connection.

Redemption.

She watched him now, the truth pressing tighter around her chest like armour that didn't fit.

Soon, he would know.

Why she was here. What she'd been hiding.

What she had planned

before he ever spoke her name.

And when that moment came— there would be only two outcomes:

He would trust her.

Or

he would kill her.

Chapter 9 – The Woman She Became

The first thing she remembered was the sound.

Not screams.

Not gunfire.

Just silence.

The kind that comes after something is erased— after a life, a name, a history no longer exists.

She was just a girl when her world vanished.

Her family wasn't part of the system. They fought it.

A resistance cell— small, buried, stubborn.

Hidden in the underbelly of a city ruled by something unseen.

They thought they were careful. They thought they had time.

They were wrong.

The retaliation wasn't just swift— it was surgical.

No bodies.

No records.

Just... gone.

A message, written in absence. She barely escaped.

Not because she was lucky.

Because they didn't think she mattered.

She spent years surviving on instinct, on hunger, on the taste of ash. Vengeance wasn't enough. She didn't want blood for blood.

She wanted to burn the machine that built the executioners.

But you couldn't kill something invisible.

You had to become invisible first.

So, she learned.

No mentors.

No family. No maps.

She made herself.

She studied systems—how power flowed, how it cloaked itself.

She crafted identities. Planted whispers.

Built stories that didn't exist until she needed them to. She became a ghost.

Not lost—designed.

She learned to navigate the liminal places: Where the elite made decisions,

and the forgotten carried them out.

And all the while, one truth remained: The assassins were the key.

She chased them for years.

The ones who killed for the Order.

Most were disposable. Silent. Buried. Erased.

But then—she found him.

A man with no past. No traceable life.

A ghost so perfectly sculpted, even those who used him likely never met him.

He was different.

And that made him valuable. She didn't expect to care.

He was a tool.

A key.

A door.

She would drag him into the light. Break his programming.

Turn him against the ones who built him.

That was the plan.

But now?

Now she wasn't sure.

Because he wasn't just a killer. He was becoming.

Something lost. Something aware.

And that—that was the one thing she hadn't accounted for. She watched him from across the room.

He didn't know. Not yet.

Didn't know who she was. Didn't know why she was here.

But soon— he would.

And when that moment came, he would see her for what she truly was.

An enemy.

He would hate her. And if she flinched— if she hesitated—it would all fall apart.

But she wasn't stopping. Not now.

Not when she was this close.

She would burn the Order to the ground.

And if he got in the way?

She would do what she must. Even if it destroyed them both.

Chapter 10 – The Unfinished Order

The encrypted device buzzed in his hand. A new contract.

No message.

No reprimand.

No explanation for the one he erased.

Just a name.

A location.

A deadline.

This wasn't forgiveness.

It was a test.

A trap.

The Order was watching.

And they were done being subtle. The target was mid-level.

Corporate. Connected.

Not a politician. Not a CEO.

But someone with access.

Someone whose death would ripple—quietly.

The job was simple. One clean shot.

One erased life.

Just like all the others. But this time...he felt it.

That same hesitation.

The fracture that had made him delete the last order.

He didn't tell her. He couldn't.

Because this wasn't about the target. It was about him.

About control.

Obedience.

Ownership.

He planned the hit with muscle memory.

Calculated.

Cold.

Trying to forget the pressure in his chest.

This is just a job, he told himself.

This is what you do.

But then—chaos.

Gunfire erupted. Not his.

A strike team burst from the shadows.

Military-trained. Coordinated.

Unfamiliar.

Not Order operatives. Someone else.

He moved before thought caught up.

Dropped two. Silenced the third.

Watched the fourth run.

By then, the target was gone.

The job was unfinished. Again.

And this time... he knew.

He was the test.

The Order hadn't cared if the executive died. They'd wanted to see if he would pull the trigger.

And he hadn't.

Not because of ethics. Not because of weakness.

But because the war wasn't clear anymore. He didn't know what side he was on.

When he returned to the safehouse, she noticed.

Of course she did.

"Something went wrong," she said.

Not a question.

A fact.

He didn't answer. She watched.

Waited.

He wanted to tell her everything.

The contract.

The ambush.

The unravelling.

But he didn't.

Because part of him— a dangerous part—still didn't know what he wanted. The Order wouldn't let this go.

He had failed them.

Twice.

He wasn't a tool anymore. He was a problem.

And the only thing worse than a disobedient asset—was one that started asking questions.

Chapter 11 – The Woman's War

The city moved like a machine— lights pulsing, crowds shifting,

power humming beneath the surface.

She moved through it like she belonged.

Slipping between shadows. Becoming part of the current.

While the hitman unravelled, she was already two steps ahead. The Order was watching him.

But they didn't know—she was watching them. She wasn't alone.

She had built something of her own. Contacts scattered through the underworld.

Hackers who broke firewalls that shouldn't exist. Ex-operatives who once believed in something,

before the Order bled it out of them. They didn't know her full plan.

No one did.

But they trusted her. Because she got results.

And now—she needed results more than ever.

She had spent years tracking the Order: their influence, their recruits, their ghosts.

Most assassins left no trail. But even ghosts leave echoes. There were patterns.

How they were chosen. How they vanished.

Where they broke.

And all of it led to one truth:

They weren't hired.

They were made.

Carefully selected. Conditioned from childhood.

Raised with one purpose:

No past.

No attachments.

No future beyond the next kill.

And now—she had a name.

Buried in encrypted files.

Scrubbed from every known archive.

A shadow behind the curtain. The one who created him.

She could tell him. Rip off the blindfold.

Show him what he really was.

But she knew what would happen.

If he learned too soon—if she didn't control how it unfolded— He would break.

Completely.

Or worse…he would never forgive her.

So, she waited.

Kept moving.

Kept watching.

Kept hoping she'd have time to choose the right moment.

But the Order had already made their move.

They had been patient. Precise.

Quiet.

And now?

They were done waiting.

They weren't just coming for him.

They were coming for her.

Chapter 12 – The Order Strikes Back

The safehouse was silent. A rare, fragile stillness.

The hitman sat in the corner, lost in a private war— unfinished contracts, fractured loyalty, an identity coming undone.

She sat across from him. Watching.

Waiting.

She knew the truth was closing in. But she wasn't ready to tell it.

And he wasn't ready to hear it.

The choice, she knew, would soon be taken from them both. He felt it before he saw it.

A shift in the city's rhythm.

Too quiet.

Too controlled.

Pedestrians moved faster. No idle chatter.

Fewer cars.

Shadows—where there shouldn't be shadows. This wasn't paranoia.

This was a hunt.

The Order was coming.

The first strike hit without warning.

Not sound—light.

A blinding white flash. Then the shatter of glass. The ceiling groaned.

Walls buckled.

Air cracked.

Drones swept through the windows like razors. Gunfire followed.

Not a warning. Not a scare tactic.

This was a message: Eradicate. Not retrieve.

They ran.

Barely.

Through rain-slick alleys. Across rusted rooftops.

Into the maze beneath the city's skin.

The city blurred around them— a smear of glass and ghosts.

But every path was blocked. Every exit predicted.

Every step known before he took it.

And for the first time in years, he felt it: Exposed.

And that terrified him more than the bullets.

They were cornered.

A dead-end loading bay.

No doors.

No light.

Just shadows tightening like nooses.

Figures closing in. Weapons raised.

And then—the city blinked.

Power grids collapsed. Surveillance died.

The drones dropped

like metal insects cut from a string. Silence fell.

And in the darkness—she moved.

Not frantic.

Not surprised.

Trained. He turned.

She was already at the terminal. Hands flying.

Eyes scanning systems.

Commanding.

Not reacting.

Not caught in this.

Orchestrating it.

She wasn't just a survivor. She was a strategist.

A soldier.

A ghost

built differently.

This wasn't coincidence. This was her world too.

They escaped.

Finally.

An abandoned freight terminal.

Dark.

Cold.

Empty.

He leaned against the wall, breathing hard.

But inside?

His mind had never been clearer. She had lied.

Not about everything.

Just the one thing that mattered.

He turned.

Eyes cold.

Voice steady.

"Who are you?"

The Order had failed— twice.

The next time, they wouldn't.

And now, he didn't just question them. He questioned her.

And he didn't know if he was more afraid of losing her—

or of finding out he never really had her at all

Chapter 13 – The Confrontation

The underground freight terminal was silent. Not just quiet—waiting.

Dust clung to the air.

Metal groaned beneath the weight of the world above.

And between them—a truth neither could outrun.

They had escaped.

But the chase had ended. Now came the reckoning.

He turned to her. Voice low.

Controlled.

Too controlled.

"Who are you?"

She had expected this. Planned for it.

But that didn't mean she was ready.

"Does it matter?"

Her tone—measured. Careful.

Deflective.

Trying to turn him back toward the enemy they shared. But he wasn't letting go.

"You knew about the ambush."

He stepped closer. Not hostile.

Just certain.

"You cut the grid.

You moved like you've done this before."

His voice—cold steel wrapped in fire.

"You're not just some woman who stumbled into my life."

She didn't deny it. She didn't speak. Didn't have to.

"You've been playing me." A breath. A beat.

"Since the beginning."

She exhaled.

Ran a hand through her hair. No more games.

She met his eyes. Direct.

Unflinching.

"I know who made you."

The words hit like a kill shot.

He didn't move. Didn't blink.

But something inside fractured.

She didn't give him everything. Not yet.

Just enough to tear open the one question he didn't know how to ask: That his life was never his.

That his orders came from ghosts. And that she—had been hunting those ghosts long before he knew they existed.

He turned away.

Hands flexed.

Fists.

Then open.

Trying to remember what he was.

"You're using me." Not with anger.

With ice.

"Just like they did."

She stepped closer. Not to comfort.

To clarify.

"Maybe I am."

No apology. Just truth.

"But I'm telling you the truth. They never did."

He didn't speak. Didn't nod.

Didn't walk away.

Just stood there— his world rewritten in six words.

He had lived his life as a weapon.

Now he didn't even know

who pulled the trigger.

But this woman? This moment?

This truth?

It was too late to walk away.

Their pasts were bound.

Their futures, uncertain. And the Order?

They weren't finished.

Not even close.

Chapter 14 – Searching for the Truth

The woman slept. He didn't.

The freight terminal echoed with quiet— the hum of distant trains,
the breath of still machinery.

Shadows crawled across the cracked ceiling. But his mind wouldn't settle.

She had told him the truth— or her version of it.

She claimed to know who made him. She said she wasn't lying.

But how could he trust that?

Trust didn't come naturally. Neither did truth.

For the first time in his life, he needed answers.

And for the first time,

he wasn't taking orders to get them.

By the time daylight bled through concrete, he was already gone.

She'd figure it out. She always did.

But this—this had to be done alone.

He moved through the city like a ghost.

Not a killer. Not a shadow.

Just a man searching for something real.

He found his lead where most wouldn't dare look— deep in the underbelly,

past codes, clearance, and fear.

A black-market broker.

The kind who trafficked in whispers and sold secrets too dangerous to name.

The meeting was tense. No one trusted ghosts—especially ones that came back from the dead.

"You're looking for something you don't want to find," the broker muttered, cigarette trembling between two scarred fingers.

"I need a name." "Names cost extra."

He gave him something better: a phrase.

Old.

Coded.

From childhood.

A verbal skeleton key—the kind only someone inside would recognize.

The broker's smirk vanished. And then—he started talking.

The Order didn't exist on paper. No agents.

No offices.

Just shadows with structure.

But the broker had seen patterns.

Digital residue.

Encryption trails too elegant to be random. Anonymous pings—recurring.

Precise.

And always, one name surfacing beneath the noise: The Architect.

The mind behind the machine.

Not just the one who gave the kill orders— the one who built the killers.

A flicker.

A fragment.

Something shifted in his memory. A voice.

Sharp. Precise.

Tight like wire.

Not a face.

Never a face.

Only commands. Only obedience.

Had he ever been free?

Or was freedom just part of the design? The broker slid a drive across the table. "You really want to know who made you?"

He nodded once. "Start here."

He reached for it—Crack.

A single shot.

Silent.

Surgical.

The broker's head snapped back. The body slumped.

A single drop of blood landed on his boot.

Warm.

Too human.

He moved

before the second shot came.

Through alleys. Onto rooftops. Melting into neon. Gone.

But the message was clear: They knew.

They were watching. They were cleaning up.

And now?

They weren't just hunting him. They were closing in.

When he returned to the safe house, she was waiting.

Not pacing.

Not afraid.

Just... still.

Arms crossed.

Eyes locked on the door. "You ran."

He didn't argue. Didn't explain.

He held up the encrypted drive.

"I think I just found the man who made me."

His voice was flat. But not cold.

And for the first time, he didn't sound like a weapon.

He sounded like a man standing at the edge of a truth that could destroy

Everything he thought was real.

Chapter 15 – The Fracture

The safe house was silent.

Too silent.

She stirred beneath the dim glow, expecting the usual signs—the shift of weight, the soft check of weapons, the breath of someone who never really slept. But there was nothing.

She sat up. Scanned the space.

His gear—gone.

His presence—erased. He had left.

No panic.

No message.

Just one long inhale. Hold.

Release.

She closed her eyes. Expected it.

Still hated it.

He'd spent his life alone. Following orders.

Surviving without attachments. Why would he change now?

Trust wasn't in his programming. Not even for her.

Maybe it wasn't just about finding answers. Maybe he didn't want her involved.

Not to protect her. Not to deceive her.

Maybe—he just didn't know how to stay.

The thought hit sharper than expected. Quieter.

Closer to the bone.

The woman she used to be wouldn't have blinked.

Mission first.

No exceptions.

That was the armour. The rule.

But this wasn't just a mission anymore.

He was never supposed to matter. A tool.

A variable.

An angle to manipulate.

She thought she was guiding him—turning him against the system that made him.

But somewhere in the chaos, he became real.

She'd seen it: The hesitation.

The cracks.

The way he looked at her— like she was something

he didn't know how to lose. And now he was gone.

Chasing shadows.

Or running from something deeper.

She paced the room. Fists tight.

Jaw tighter.

"If he wanted help, he'd have asked." That was the voice that kept her alive.

But another voice rose— quieter,

more dangerous:

What if he just doesn't know how?

She stopped moving.

Stared at the door like it might answer for him. A decision waited.

Wait?

Hope?

Trust?

No.

She wasn't the kind of girl who stayed behind.

She activated her network. Signals.

Encrypted channels.

Contact pings lighting up like ghosts returning. He thought he could vanish.

Not from her.

They were chasing the same truth now. But not together.

They were on separate paths, twisting through the wreckage of their pasts. And when those paths crossed again—they might not be on the same side.

Chapter 16 – The Decryption

The industrial sector was dead.

Rusting steel skeletons loomed overhead, their shattered windows catching the weak spill of neon.

The air smelled of oil, rust, and long-forgotten violence.

Perfect.

He didn't need comfort. Only isolation.

Tonight, he carried something too dangerous for carelessness.

The encrypted drive felt heavier than it should— not in weight, but in meaning.

This wasn't data. This was origin.

A truth buried so deep, they built him on top of it.

He moved without noise.

Found shelter in the wreckage of a disused foundry.

Hands built a closed-circuit terminal from salvaged parts, military cast-offs,

a mind sharpened by training no child should endure.

No signal.

No trace.

Only firewalls.

Only focus.

The encryption was brutal— layers on layers, armour designed to outlive empires.

But he'd been trained for this. Not just to kill.

To breach.

To hunt.

And knowledge was just another target.

One by one, the walls fell. Code surrendered.

Locks cracked.

The first decrypted file wasn't a name. It was a symbol.

He froze.

Geometric. Precise. Cruel as geometry. Colder than memory.

He had seen it before— in drills, in dreams, etched into the edges of recollection like a brand.

But he had never understood it.

Until now.

Below it, a codename blinked to life: THE ARCHITECT.

A corrupted audio file surfaced. Distorted. Fragmented.

Still intact.

He hit play.

A voice emerged— measured.

Male.

Human.

Not someone he knew.

But someone who knew him.

The words came in a language he was never taught— but understood.

Something buried in the bones of his training.

"You were designed for more than obedience." "You were meant to be permanent."

Permanent.

The word hit harder than any bullet. Cold.

Heavy. Final.

He stared at the screen, jaw clenched.

More files cracked open. A list.

Operatives.

Dozens of them.

Most names crossed out in red.

Terminated.

Erased.

Purged.

He scrolled faster.

His name should be there. It wasn't.

Why?

Then another file loaded— video. Grainy. Flickering.

Holding itself together by sheer will.

A room.

Dark. Clinical.

A shadowed figure sat at a table. Unclear.

Unnamed.

Then—a flicker of text:

Initiating Phase Two.

His pulse slowed.

His instincts screamed.

And just before the feed collapsed— one final line burned across the screen:

If he finds this, eliminate him.

Silence.

He leaned back, chest rising slow, like he could inhale enough to hold the world still.

This wasn't a breach. It wasn't a mistake.

They had always planned for this.

The second he started asking questions— they started preparing answers.

Now?

They weren't watching. They were moving.

And they were coming.

Chapter 17 - The Hunt for Him

The city pulsed beneath her feet.

Neon spilled across rain-slick pavement, voices blurring into the mechanical hum of a world that never slept.

But she wasn't listening.

He was gone.

No message.

No warning.

Just absence.

If he thought, he could disappear? He didn't know her well enough.

He was good at vanishing.

But she was better at finding what didn't want to be found.

She moved fast—pulling favours, calling in markers. Hackers. Brokers.

Ghosts who owed her more than loyalty.

Surveillance feeds. Unregistered power surges.

Flickers in the city's nervous system.

No direct leads.

But the anomalies—the ones nobody else noticed— began to align.

A heat spike in a long-dead district.

A power fluctuation in a place that should've stayed dark.

It was him.

She was closing in.

This should've been about the mission. The Order.

Revenge.

But it wasn't.

Not anymore.

Somewhere between silence and near-death, something had shifted.

She wasn't just chasing an operative. She was chasing him.

And that terrified her more than anything else ever had.

The industrial hideout was dark. Silent.

Breathing tension.

She found him hunched over a screen, face lit in the cold blue glow of decrypted secrets.

He didn't flinch.

"You should've told me."

Her voice steady. But sharp.

He didn't turn.

"I had to do this alone."

"You were never supposed to be part of this."

She stepped forward.

Boots whispering across concrete. "That's not your call."

He stared at the screen.

But she saw the tension in his shoulders— he wasn't sure anymore.

Her eyes scanned the terminal. The symbol.

The list.

All the red crosses.

It didn't take long to understand.

"They've been tracking you since the beginning."

He nodded.

Barely.

"They trained me to forget that."

"You think cutting me out protects me?"

She moved closer. No more distance. No more deflection.

"After everything?"

Finally—he turned. And for the first time, she saw it.

Not the weapon. Not the operative.

The man.

And he was breaking.

"I don't know how to do this."

The words cracked something between them. She could've stayed angry.

Should've.

It would've been easier.

Instead—she stepped in.

Her voice dropped. Quiet.

Unshakable.

"Then stop running." Silence.

He didn't answer.

But something shifted. Not surrender.

Trust.

And then—the alarms erupted. Piercing.

Urgent.

Unforgiving.

The Order had found them.

Chapter 18 - Running Together

Sirens wailed. Sharp. Closer. No more hiding. No more time.

They locked eyes. No words.

Just a silent understanding.

This was it.

Together, they ran. Through skeletal corridors. Across rusted catwalks.

Into the underbelly of a city that devours the slow.

The Order was relentless. But so were they.

They moved in sync. No signals.

No commands.

She stopped when he did.

He shifted course before she even looked.

Instinct.

Reflex.

Trust.

This wasn't just two fugitives. This was something new.

They were becoming a unit.

No one led.

No one followed.

They moved.

An abandoned high-rise. Forgotten.

Buried in shadow.

They slipped inside, every step deliberate.

Every sound accounted for.

Only when the silence returned did they stop.

Breathless.

Alive.

Still here.

But something had changed.

The silence wasn't hollow anymore. It wasn't tense.

It was full—with everything they hadn't said.

He looked at her. Not like a handler. Not like a target.

Not even like a partner.

Like someone who mattered. Someone who understood.

His entire life had been built around solitude. People were threats.

Distractions.

Obstacles.

But she...She didn't fit.

She wasn't a liability. She wasn't leverage.

She was real.

And that terrified him more than any ambush ever had.

She had come to use him. To turn the machine inward.

To break the system from within. He was supposed to be the weapon.

But here— now—he was something else.

More.

More than what they made. More than what she expected.

And she didn't want to lose him.

She moved first. Closed the distance. No hesitation.

Her voice was low. Steady.

"You don't have to do this alone."

He didn't pull away. He always had.

He didn't know how not to. But now?

Now, he didn't want to let her go.

They both knew it wouldn't last. The Order would come.

The war was still ahead.

But their paths—once parallel, then intersecting— were now bound.

This wasn't just an escape anymore.

It was a choice.

And for the first time in their lives, they would make it—together.

Not just to run.

To fight.

Chapter 19 - The Insider

The high-rise was quiet.

Neon shimmered beyond shattered windows, casting long shadows across steel bones.

They sat in silence. Backs to the wall. Eyes on the skyline.

This wasn't survival anymore. It was a countdown.

Running wouldn't save them. Fighting wouldn't be enough.

They needed something more.

Someone who knew the Order from the inside.

She spoke first. A name.

Buried. Forgotten.

A whisper passed between ghosts.

He knew it.

Thought they were dead.

"If they're still breathing," she said, "they're the only one who can tell us how to bring the Order down."

He exhaled.

Slow. Tight.

This wasn't just a name. It was a warning.

You didn't seek this person.

You survived them.

But if the name still echoed— it meant only one thing: They were still out there.

No one left the Order alive. No loose ends.

No corpses.

Just disappearance.

But she had been chasing shadows longer than he knew.

Dead message boards. Encrypted drops.

Fragments of intel from ex-operatives too scared to speak on open air.

Everything pointed to a single place— a site beyond the city's edge.

Beyond surveillance.

Beyond reach.

"We go there," he said.

"We get answers... or a trap."

The city fell behind them. Neon faded to grey.

The roads cracked beneath rusted wheels. Civilization peeled away like corroded skin.

It was just the two of them now.

Alone

with what they hadn't said.

She caught him watching her. Not like a threat.

Not like a mission.

Like he was memorizing her face—just in case.

He caught her doing the same.

If things were different...Maybe they wouldn't be just two weapons in a war.

But things weren't different.

The compound rose from the dust. Steel bones.

Cracked concrete. Half-sunken.

Half-erased.

It was too still.

His instincts locked.

That hum at the base of his skull—Wrong.

"Something's off," he said.

The air felt... filtered. Too clean.

Too quiet.

The place looked abandoned. But he knew better.

"We're not the only ones here."

Her hand moved to her weapon. No words. Just readiness.

If the Order had reached the insider first—they were already too late.

Chapter 20 - The Ally's Last Words

The compound was dead. No movement.

No sound.

Just the wind, slicing through steel bones and shattered glass.

Someone had lived here. But now?

It felt like a tomb.

They moved carefully—weapons drawn, eyes scanning every shadow. This wasn't just a hideout.

It was a trap that hadn't sprung. Yet.

He felt it before he heard it— a voice, low and gravel-edged. Calm. Inevitable.

"You shouldn't have come."

A figure stepped from the dark. Older than expected.

Lean. Hardened.

Eyes like ground glass.

They weren't surprised. Not at him.

They'd been waiting.

This wasn't just a ghost.

This was what he might've become if he'd seen too much and survived it.

No greetings.

No games.

"You want to bring them down?"

"Then you need to know what you are."

The words hit like a blade— quiet, but deep.

The Order hadn't trained assassins.

They engineered them.

Even the resistance—the uprisings, the martyrs, the chaos— was part of the model.

Designed opposition. Controlled rebellion. An excuse for control.

But hers?

Her family's?

They weren't part of the simulation. They slipped through.

Barely.

And they paid for it in blood.

"The Architect," the ally said, "isn't a person."

"It's a system."

A program built to sculpt killers from childhood. No names.

No memories.

Just precision. Purpose. Permanence.

Everything—the detachment, the gaps, the reflexes— wasn't instinct.

It was architecture.

He had never been free. Not once.

She stood still.

Silent.

Listening.

This wasn't just his reckoning. It was hers too.

Because the same system that destroyed her family...created him.

The first bullet shattered the window. Glass exploded.

The room became war.

The Order had arrived. Fast. Surgical.

No warning.

No mercy.

The ally didn't flinch. They moved fast— grabbed his wrist, shoved something into his palm.

"This is everything."

"You want to end them? Use it."

A small chip. Light as a breath.

Heavy as a loaded gun.

No time for questions. No time for goodbyes.

The ally turned— fired.

One operative dropped. Then another.

But there were too many.

A clean shot— centre mass.

The ally staggered.

Blood bloomed across their chest like ink on cracked paper.

They slid to the floor. No scream.

No panic.

Just one sharp breath— and a look that said: This was the plan.

They didn't die afraid.

They died giving him a chance.

Gunfire chased them into the wasteland. The compound burned behind them.

He didn't look back. He didn't need to.

In his fist, the data chip burned like a brand.

Not just information. Not just leverage.

The key.

The truth.

The final card in the game.

But in his chest— not just fury.

Grief.

Not for the ally.

For the life he never got to live.

She watched him from across the broken road. No words.

But she felt it— something had changed.

Before, he was chasing answers.

Now?

He was hunting an ending.

"We finish this," he said. Voice low.

Final.

And for the first time in his life— he wasn't following orders.

He was giving one.

Chapter 21 - The Final Test

The stolen data chip sat between them, its brushed steel casing catching the flicker of a dying light.

So small.

So ordinary.

Yet it held everything.

Names.

Codes.

Commands.

The blueprint of the machine that built him. The key to burning it all down.

But he didn't look at it.

His eyes were somewhere else— deep, distant, haunted by the ally's final words: "You were designed for more than obedience." "You were meant to be permanent."

What did that mean?

She watched him from across the room. Not with suspicion.

Not with strategy. With concern.

Something was shifting in him. Not a breakdown.

A reckoning.

"Talk to me," she said. Quiet.

No edge.

No command.

He didn't respond. Fists curled.

Jaw clenched.

He wasn't breaking. He was rewriting.

Not a soldier. Not a killer.

A product.

He stepped into the night.

The city pulsed around him—dying neon, flickering signs, synthetic wind.

But inside?

Only silence.

He walked without direction—only the weight of everything he'd never questioned.

His life had been clean.

Precise.

One directive at a time.

Never why. Never who. Just go.

Kill.

Disappear.

And now?

Now that the orders had stopped… he didn't know who he was.

His feet led him to a memory.

A recruitment site.

One of the Order's seedbeds. Still running.

Quiet.

Efficient.

Inside: the next generation. Teenagers.

Children.

No names.

No pasts.

Just movement. Perfect. Flawless. Like his had been.

He watched from the dark— a phantom among phantoms.

Was this what he escaped?

Or what he was meant to end?

He could vanish. Disappear again.

Let someone else fight.

But if he did?

The machine would keep building. More ghosts.

More killers.

More stolen futures. No.

He wasn't just a product.

He was proof the system could break. "You were meant to be permanent."

Not a warning.

A challenge.

He returned just before dawn.

She looked up from the shadows, saw his silhouette framed in cracked concrete and cold light.

He didn't have to speak. But he did.

"We burn them to the ground."

Not for revenge. Not for her.

Not even for himself.

For the ones still trapped.

For the ones who hadn't chosen.

She nodded. Not in surprise. But in solidarity. Respect.

Maybe something more. They said nothing else.

Together, they plugged in the data chip. The screen flickered.

Encrypted code unfolded—line by line, like a dying thing fighting to live.

Names.

Coordinates.

Fail-safes.

Truth.

Every root. Every room. Every kill switch. All of it.

The war wasn't coming.

It had already begun.

Chapter 22 - Unravelling the Order

The data chip sat in the terminal. Silent. Unassuming.

Until the screen flickered to life. Then everything changed.

Lines of encrypted files unfurled— slow at first,

then like a dam breaking.

Schematics. Financial records. Operative rosters. Kill lists.

Not just contracts.

Blueprints.

They stood shoulder to shoulder, motionless. Because this wasn't just intel.

This was truth.

The kind too big to carry.

The kind too dangerous to ignore. The Order wasn't a syndicate.

Wasn't a network.

It was a machine— cold, precise, systemic.

Hardwired into the foundation of global power. Invisible, but omnipresent.

They didn't answer to a single man.

The Architect wasn't a person. It was a system— a predictive framework. An algorithm of influence, embedded in governments, mega corps, defence networks—even the news cycle.

Decisions weren't made. They were modelled.

And anyone who deviated from the model?

Erased.

Corporate titans. Government leaders. Rebels.

Journalists.

For decades, the Order had sculpted history— through assassination and omission.

They didn't just eliminate threats. They rewrote reality.

And at the centre? Not a face.

Not a singular will. A council.

Rotating.

Invisible.

Untouchable.

He hadn't served a master. He'd served an empire.

She leaned in.

Fingers hovered above the screen, tracing names burned into her memory.

Names she didn't know— but had always suspected.

Names that filled the gaps in every loss she could never explain.

"They built this," she said. Low. Precise. Final.

"They destroyed everything—for control."

Vengeance had fuelled her for years. But now?

Now she had ignition.

He stared at the files like a man reading his own obituary.

Every mission.

Every kill.

Mapped. Modelled. Chosen.

Not by chance. Not by contract. By design.

"I was never supposed to ask questions," he said.

Because he was never meant to know. That was the real contract.

But now?

Now he held the blade. And for the first time, it was pointed the right way.

Buried deep in the data: a weakness.

A central hub.

The convergence point for the Order's communications, intel, and financial control systems.

Destroy it— and the machine collapses.

But it wouldn't be clean.

It wouldn't be quiet.

It was fortified.

Multi-layered.

Guarded by operatives trained to anticipate every tactic—even his.

This wasn't a mission. It was a war.

They gathered what remained: gear, weapons, stolen blueprints stitched together from the inside out.

But they weren't going alone.

She sent the signal. Out to the forgotten. The discarded.

The exiled.

The broken.

Ghosts who once lived in the Order's shadow. Ex-operatives.

Burned assets.

Survivors too dangerous to kill, but too silent to leave behind.

They came.

Not for redemption. Not for revenge.

But for a chance—to matter.

For a moment, the world held its breath. The silence before fire.

He turned to her. Voice low.

Steady.

"If we do this… we don't walk away clean." She didn't flinch.

"I was never looking for clean."

A pause.

Not hesitation.

Just clarity.

Trust.

Maybe something more.

And for the first time in his life, he didn't want to do it alone.

They stepped into the night.

The city pulsed around them, still dreaming.

But the air had shifted. Subtle. Charged.

The silence before collapse.

And somewhere, deep within the Order's architecture, the algorithm registered it: A deviation.

A tremor.

Someone was coming.

He gripped his weapon. Exhaled once.

No more orders. No more masks.

No more hesitation. Only the end.

Of the people who made him.

Of the system that erased them both.

This time, they chose the fight.

And they wouldn't stop

until it was finished.

Chapter 23 - Walking into the Fire

The city moved like a machine— steel and neon, faceless and endless. But they weren't part of it anymore.

They walked through the crowd like ghosts. Eyes fixed.

Steps silent.

Purpose humming beneath their skin.

They weren't running. They were hunting.

What didn't they know? They were already prey.

The underground had given them everything: Access codes.

Entry points.

Intel mapped down to the meter.

The plan was clear: Infiltrate. Destroy the core.

Erase the Order from existence.

But the deeper they moved into the city's steel skeleton, the more something pulled at him—a wrongness in the quiet.

This was the Order's heart.

There should've been drones. Guards. Surveillance. Instead—nothing.

She felt it too.

Her hand drifted toward her weapon. "Either we're better than we thought…"

She didn't finish the sentence. Because they both knew— this wasn't victory.

It was invitation.

And it was too late to turn back.

They breached the perimeter. No resistance.

No alarms.

No lockdowns.

Just a building—waiting.

Inside, the silence thickened. They reached the sanctum: the pulsing heart of the Order's network.

Rows of servers stood like monoliths.

A single command terminal at the centre.

He moved toward it, calm and precise. She scanned the shadows, pulse steady.

Then—the monitors came alive.

Not security feeds. Not diagnostics.

A room.

A boardroom.

Figures seated in darkness—watching.

Then a voice crackled to life. Measured. Smooth.

Laced with something close to amusement.

"You've come so far. And for what?

To burn something, you never understood?"

He froze.

That voice—not just from training drills.

Deeper. Personal.

"Who are you?"

A low chuckle.

Familiar.

Intimate.

"You know who I am."

The monitors cleared. Static dissolved.

A face emerged.

Older. Sharper. Unmistakable.

Not just a handler. Not just a mentor.

The Architect.

The only person he ever trusted. His voice dropped—cold. Flat. "You."

"Did you think we didn't account for this? You're not the first to resist.

You're not even the first to get this far." The truth landed like a blade.

This wasn't revolution. It was protocol.

The Order didn't fear rebellion. They designed it.

Every collapse? Controlled. Every insurgent? Scripted. Every betrayal? Anticipated.

She turned to him.

Eyes wide—not with fear. With fury.

"They knew."

"This wasn't about ending them.

It was about making us believe we could."

The floor vibrated.

A low hum rising beneath them.

"You are not the first," the Architect said. "But you will be the last."

The detonation hit like thunder.

Steel screamed. Concrete split.

The ceiling began to collapse.

They ran.

Not in retreat— in defiance.

The Order didn't want survivors. They wanted silence.

Erasure.

But they miscalculated. Again.

They thought this would end it.

They thought they still held the narrative.

But as fire chased them through the dying halls, he didn't feel fear.

Not even rage.

Only clarity.

Cold. Focused. Unforgiving.

The Order thought they were gods. They thought they had already won.

But they made one mistake—They let him live long enough to learn the truth.

And now?

He wasn't walking away. He was walking back—to finish what they started.

Chapter 24 - Running Through Fire

The walls shuddered.

Explosions tore through steel and concrete. Detonations rolled like thunder—shaking the bones of the fortress.

Smoke.

Fire.

The shriek of metal giving way.

They didn't hesitate. They ran.

A blur of motion through collapsing corridors. Flames curling.

Ceilings cracking.

Concrete breaking underfoot.

Every second— a calculation.

Every breath— a borrowed one.

The hitman led them, his instincts carving a path through chaos. Fastest route.

Fewest risks. Always forward.

But this wasn't just survival anymore. Every decision he made—he made for her, too.

And she followed. No hesitation.

No questions.

Only trust.

But even she knew— this was bad.

The intercom crackled.

A voice sliced through the smoke.

Smooth. Calm. Detached.

"Still running?"

"There is no escape from what you are."

He didn't flinch. Didn't look back.

Just clenched his fists— and kept moving.

The main exit: gone. Blocked.

Steel and rubble twisted like shattered bones.

Only one way left: Up.

They bolted for the stairwell. Feet pounding.

Lungs burning.

The building groaned, each floor a ticking fuse.

They reached the top. Windows blown out.

The city sprawled beneath them— a chaos of sirens and smoke.

"We jump," he said.

His voice was calm. Too calm.

She stared. "We what—?" No time.

He grabbed her hand. And they jumped.

The wind tore the breath from their lungs. Vertigo hit like a freight train.

Weightless.

Soundless.

Then—impact.

A nearby rooftop.

Hard. Brutal. Unforgiving.

They rolled.

Skidded.

Bodies screaming.

And then—boom.

The fortress behind them erupted. A thunderclap of flame and steel. The sky lit up in fire.

Glass shattered for blocks. The city shook.

They lay still.

Gasping.

Alive.

She turned to him. Eyes wide.

Breathing.

Then—a sharp, breathless laugh. Half fury. Half awe.

"If you ever do that again—" He cut her off. Voice ragged. Quiet.

"We're alive."

Not just a fact.

A declaration.

A revelation.

They stared at the blaze.

The fortress—gone. But the war?

Still waiting.

The real power hadn't fallen. It had vanished.

Buried itself deeper. Stronger.

Smarter.

She turned to him. Her voice soft.

Certain.

"We're not ghosts anymore."

He nodded.

Jaw tight.

Eyes like steel.

"No," he said. "We finish this."

Not for revenge. Not for the past.

Not for what they lost.

For whom they chose to become.

For whom they refused to forget.

For the ones still trapped in the fire

they finally walked through.

Chapter 25 - Into the Shadows

Behind them, the city burned. Twisted steel. Shattered glass. A monument to destruction.

But there was no victory.

Only silence. Smoke. Aftermath.

The Order's headquarters was gone. But the war?

It was just beginning.

They didn't look back. Didn't hesitate.

They vanished into the cracks of the city— Ghosts before the flames even settled.

The response came fast. Too fast.

Lockdowns. Checkpoints. Drones in formation.

Every contact—burned.

Every safehouse—compromised. Every backdoor—sealed shut.

They weren't being hunted. They were being erased.

They slipped into the city's underbelly, finding shelter in a forgotten resistance bunker buried deep in the sewer veins.

Dark. Rotting. Heavy with the ghosts of failed rebellions.

It wasn't a home.

It was a grave someone else never got out of.

And they both knew—They wouldn't be hiding long.

He had spent his life preparing for anything. Kill the target. Erase the evidence. Disappear.

But this— No mission. No handler.

No objective but survival— This was something else.

He was ready for every possibility except this one:

Fighting for himself.

She didn't spiral.

She moved.

Encrypted channels. Phantom contacts.

Flickers of rebellion still alive in broken code and buried names.

She didn't hesitate. And he saw it— The shift.

She wasn't just surviving. She was leading.

And for the first time— He let her.

Weapons – stolen from caches before the Order could scorch them.

Allies – outliers still hiding, still angry, still waiting.

Intel – the chip wasn't the only truth. There were more threads to pull.

Everything they had left— It would be enough.

Because next time the Order came? They wouldn't run.

Silence filled the bunker. Not peace.

Not safety. But stillness.

She watched him across the room. Saw the tension in his frame.

The way he still hadn't put down his weapon.

"You've always fought for someone else," she said. Voice quiet. Steady.

"This time, fight for you."

He looked at her.

Really looked.

And for the first time, he didn't feel like a tool. He felt like a man.

The distance between them?

It wasn't about safety anymore. It was about choice.

The Order would come. They knew it.

Counted on it.

But this time, there would be no ambush.

This time—they would choose the battlefield.

She loaded a stolen rifle, eyes cold and clear. "Let's end this."

He nodded, checking his gear. "No more waiting."

No more orders. No more shadows. Only the end.

The Order thought they'd buried the rebellion. Thought they'd erased the ghosts.

But ghosts don't die. They haunt.

And now?

They were done hiding.

The war had a pulse again.

And it was coming straight for the ones who started it.

Chapter 26 – The Final Trap

The stolen terminal cast a pale blue glow across the bunker.

Lines of code danced on cracked concrete. Maps. Encrypted files. City schematics.

The war lived here now quiet and coiled.

They didn't have an army. They didn't need one.

They had the Order's arrogance.

Buried in the wreckage of burned archives— a location.

A so-called neutral zone.

Never documented. Never spoken aloud.

A central node where top-tier commanders met in the open.

Untouchable. Invisible. Until now.

They weren't going in guns blazing. That's what the Order expected.

Instead?

They would pull the Order to them.

One carefully seeded message: A false intel drop.

"The hitman is alive. Unarmed. Waiting for pickup."

They wouldn't ignore it. They couldn't.

They'd send teams. Maybe even handlers. Maybe even the ones who made him.

And when they came?

They'd walk straight into a kill zone.

She took the digital front. Hacked the power grid.

Hijacked surveillance networks.

Turned the city's own infrastructure against itself.

He handled the streets. Claymores in alleyways.

Sniper nests on rooftops.

Explosives buried under manholes and intersections. Every path became a coffin.

As soon as the fake drop hit the dark net, the reaction was instant.

Encrypted chatter. Mobilization codes. Shadows moving.

Just as planned. It was working.

Outside, the city buzzed with synthetic light and distant sirens.

Inside?

Stillness.

He cleaned his weapons. She monitored the feeds.

They didn't speak—until she did.

"If we do this... there's no coming back."

Her voice didn't shake. But it carried weight.

He looked at her.

And for once, there was no war in his eyes. Just her.

"I never planned on coming back."

But now?

There was something worth surviving for.

The monitors flared. Convoys. Black SUVs.

Drones slicing across rooftops. Strike teams. Heavy. Fast.

She smirked.

"Right on schedule."

He stepped into position. Calm. Precise.

Finger resting on the detonator.

No more ghosts. No more doubts. Only the end.

Engines growled beyond the buildings. The hum of the city shifted, quieter.

More expectant.

He exhaled.

Eyes fixed on the kill zone. "Let's see how gods bleed."

Chapter 27 – The Price of War

The Order took the bait. Exactly as planned.

Their elite teams rolled into the kill zone— Confident. Controlled.

Arrogant.

And then—Detonation.

Explosives lit the street in fire and steel. Armoured trucks flipped like toys.

Sniper fire punched through helmets before commands could be given.

Surveillance feeds died. Comms went silent.

Panic surged through the ranks.

For the first time—the Order wasn't hunting. They were prey.

And the hitman?

He wasn't holding back anymore.

The counterattack came fast— But fractured. Sloppy.

They were trained for rebellion. Not reckoning.

This wasn't just an ambush. It was a message.

The woman watched the lines collapse. Fires blooming in the dark.

She smirked.

"Look at them run."

The Order—once untouchable— Now?

Running scared.

But then— Everything shifted.

His comms crackled. Static.

Nothing.

Worse than an explosion. Worse than a scream.

She was covering his flank. Holding the line.

Now— Silence.

Then it came: A voice.

Distorted. Cold. Controlled.

"Stand down." "We have her."

His breath caught.

The battlefield blurred.

Smoke. Fire. Bodies. None of it mattered.

Then—movement.

A black SUV slicing through the chaos. A flash in the backseat.

Her.

Fighting.

Shouting.

Then—the door slammed shut. Gone.

The victory?

Ash.

The war, the vengeance, the blood? Forgotten.

Now—There was only her.

The Architect's voice slithered through the air. Mocking. Calm. Triumphant.

"You were never going to win this way."

"Did you really think brute force was enough?"

His fists clenched. Teeth grinding.

They wanted him angry. Wanted him reckless.

Then—The dagger.

"Come to us. Alone." "Or she dies."

He stood in the ruin of his own making. Survivor of traps, betrayals, kill lists.

But this?

This was the one thing he had never trained for.

Caring.

Choosing.

The old version of him? He would've vanished. Cut losses.

Survived.

But that version was dead. She changed that.

She made him feel again. Made him real.

And now?

Now they made their mistake.

They thought they'd set the trap. But they gave him something else:

A reason.

He gripped his weapon. Eyes hard.

Heart locked.

"If they want a trap…" "…they just walked into one."

Chapter 28 – The Counter Move

The battlefield was silent. Smoke curled from wreckage. Ash drifted like falling glass.

Gunpowder hung in the air—thick, metallic, final.

He stood alone. She was gone. Taken.

The only person who ever looked at him and didn't just see

a weapon.

Didn't flinch at what he was. Saw who he was.

The man he used to be would've disappeared. Cut his losses.

Survived.

But that man?

He was already dead.

And if the Order thought he'd walk into their fortress unarmed, begging for mercy?

They didn't understand the game. Not anymore.

This wasn't about sacrifice. This was about leverage.

About fear. About control.

They needed to believe one thing: He was more dangerous with her alive than dead.

So, he gave them what they wanted—The illusion of surrender.

He accessed the last encrypted cache from the burned war room.

Buried intel. Black sites. Personnel. The Architects were still shadows. But their operatives?

They bled like everyone else.

One name surfaced. A regional director.

Mid-command. High clearance. Operational authority.

Important.

And most importantly?

Trackable.

He sent the message.

Short. Deceptive. Quietly desperate.

"I'll come alone. I'll give myself up. Just let her live."

The response came fast. Too fast.

"Good choice."

They thought they'd won. Again.

While they celebrated, he hunted. Like they trained him to.

Silent. Precise. Efficient.

One chokehold.

One chemical injection.

One bound, unconscious commander in the trunk of a stolen car.

He took a photo.

Time-stamped. Geo-verified.

Then—He hijacked their private channel. Direct line. No firewalls. No layers.

The voice that answered? Cold. Measured. Familiar.

"You've made a mistake." He didn't blink.

"No. You did."

He slid the image across the feed. Proof of life.

Proof of leverage.

Silence.

Heavy.

Then— "What do you want?" He lit a cigarette.

Calm. Controlled. Coiled.

"Her. Alive. Unharmed." A beat.

"And if we refuse?"

He smiled.

A predator's smile.

"Then this man dies screaming."

This wasn't a deal.

It wasn't even a threat. It was a declaration.

He was no longer a rogue asset. No longer a ghost in their machine.

He was a player.

With pieces of his own.

The woman's fate still hung in the balance. The Order still held cards.

But now?

So did he.

And if they thought this would end clean— They hadn't learned a thing.

Because the worst thing you can do to a weapon is make it feel.

Now?

They'd built something they couldn't control. And it was coming for them.

Chapter 29 – The Ultimatum

He waited.

Still.

Controlled.

Unshaken.

The Order wouldn't respond right away. He knew that.

They didn't panic. They calculated.

Right now, they were running models. Risk algorithms.

Contingency paths.

They were asking the wrong questions: How fast could they locate him?

Could they eliminate him and recover the commander before the damage spread?

They weren't used to being cornered. But this wasn't about control anymore.

He wasn't a rogue asset. He was a threat.

The first message came through. Encrypted. Short. Predictable.

"We don't do trades. You of all people should know that."

He smiled.

A delay tactic. Classic. They were stalling.

Buying time.

Let them try.

Let them believe they still held the board.

The second message hit minutes later. Different tone.

Sharper.

"You can't win this. Even if you kill him, we'll replace him. You think this gives you power? It only delays the inevitable."

He stared at the screen. Unmoved.

Then calmly uploaded the clip.

The commander. Bound.

Bruised.

Eyes wide with real fear.

No filters.

No edits.

Just humiliation.

A mirror they weren't ready to investigate.

Then— A pause.

A new voice.

Lower. Measured. Real authority.

"What do you want?"

There it was.

Not anger.

Not pride.

Fear.

He leaned into the mic. Calm. Precise.

Surgical.

"Neutral ground. No surveillance. One for one."

Silence.

The long kind.

The kind that lets you hear pressure cracking. Then:

"And if we say no?"

He turned the mic.

Let the click of the safety echo through the channel. "Then I'll make you watch."

No threats.

No shouting.

Just truth.

He could feel it now.

The tension in their silence. The sweat behind the static.

This wasn't a negotiation. It was an exposure.

And they couldn't afford it. Not after everything.

So, they folded.

A time.

A place.

Coordinates delivered like a death sentence.

But he wasn't a fool. This wasn't surrender. It was a trap.

The difference this time?

He would be the one springing it.

He ran the checklist again. Surveillance sweep.

Sniper cover. Escape routes.

Contingency for the contingency.

Still—None of it answered the question gnawing at him. Would she be alive when he got there?

He didn't know.

But he would burn the world to find out.

Chapter 30 – The Order's Real Game

The industrial zone was silent.

Steel bones. Long-dead machines. The hum of engines growing louder.

He stood in the centre. Still. Ready. Waiting.

At his feet, the Order's regional commander. Bound. Gagged. Breathing shallow.

Just a bargaining chip. Nothing more.

The convoy rolled in.

Black vehicles. Windows tinted like secrets. No urgency. No fear. Just confidence.

This wasn't a negotiation. It was performance.

His instincts flared.

The operatives moved too smoothly. Too rehearsed.

They didn't look like a rescue team. They looked like undertakers.

His hand brushed the grip of his pistol. Something was wrong.

Then—He saw her.

Dragged from the lead vehicle. Two enforcers at her side.

Bruised. Restrained. But standing.

Still defiant.

Their eyes met for a breath. One heartbeat.

No words.

Warning.

She didn't speak. She didn't need to.

Her look said everything: It's a trap.

A figure stepped forward. Sharp suit. Steady stride. Calm. Smiling.

The Order's representative. A voice like oil over glass.

"Is this your idea of a negotiation?" The hitman's response was razor flat.

"Walk away with your man. Or die here." The representative didn't blink.

Instead—He stepped closer. Smiling wider.

"You still don't get it." "This was never about her."

He gestured to the scene. The vehicles. The perimeter. The sniper glints.

"This was always about you."

The chill hit hard. Not just cold clarity.

They weren't here to retrieve anyone. This wasn't a trade.

It was a purge.

"You were a weapon," the man said. "But now? You're a liability."

Then— One shot.

The commander at his feet dropped. Dead before the echo faded.

The Order executed their own. No leverage.

No hesitation.

The message was crystal: No deals. No mercy. No mistakes.

He moved— Too late.

Red dots lit his chest.

Snipers. Drones. Enforcers already in motion. Every exit sealed.

This wasn't a standoff. This was a kill box.

Then— Her voice.

Distant. Urgent. A warning.

A trigger.

But the bullets drowned it out. Gunfire cracked.

Drones screamed. The ground lit up.

He returned fire. Precise. Deadly. Every shot earned.

If he was going down— He wasn't going alone.

But somewhere deeper—beneath instinct, beneath rage— He knew something else: This wasn't the end.

Not yet.

Because while they watched him— While they underestimated her—

She was already moving.

Chapter 31 – Turning the Trap

The hitman stood in the open. Surrounded.

Nowhere to go.

Weapons raised.

Fingers tight on triggers. Seconds from death.

She was still in their grip. Bruised. Bloody. Silent.

But not afraid.

She watched him—eyes sharp, unflinching. And then—A flick of her hand. Barely a movement.

A signal.

He saw it.

Understood it.

She hadn't been captured. She'd been waiting.

BOOM.

An explosion ripped through the air. Then another.

And another.

Order vehicles erupted in flame— Steel twisted, fire rolled, screams echoed.

Shockwaves staggered the enforcers. Gunfire paused—just long enough. She moved.

Twisting out of their grip, elbow snapping one jaw— grabbing a falling weapon mid-motion.

Two shots.

Two bodies.

Down.

His cue.

Instant.

He launched forward— not to run.

To kill.

They weren't ready.

The trap had turned inside out.

He was a phantom with teeth.

His movements: cold, brutal, exact.

Not just escape.

Revenge.

Every shot sent a message:

You should've killed me when you had the chance.

She moved beside him— not behind.

With him.

Her fire matched his.

They were fury, tandem and timed.

A path opened in blood and smoke.

A vehicle waited—unlocked, still intact.

They dove inside.

Drones buzzed overhead. Bullets tore the sky.

Tires screamed. They vanished.

Miles away. Silence.

A hidden bunker buried in concrete and dark. No comms. No signals. Off-grid.

They sat in the stillness. Breathing. Bleeding. Alive.

And then— Laughter.

Hers.

Sharp. Bitter. Disbelieving. "That was your plan?"

He gripped the wheel. Exhaled slowly.

Didn't smile.

But his eyes said enough.

For the first time in a long time— He felt alive.

She studied him.

Voice low. Calm. Certain. "They won't stop."

He looked at her.

Eyes dark. Purpose clear. "Neither will we."

No more traps.

No more hesitation. Next time?

The Order bleeds first.

Chapter 32 – The Order's Last Move

The streets were silent. No sirens. No pursuit.

Just silence.

And that made it worse.

They moved through shadows— watching rooftops, scanning the sky. Every footstep laced with tension.

Waiting for the next bullet. But it never came.

The Order wasn't chasing them. They had stopped hunting.

They were containing.

Checkpoints on every block. Drones circling like vultures.

Facial recognition woven into every glass pane. The air itself felt watched.

Every ally?

Gone.

Not dead.

Erased.

As if they never existed.

The trap failed.

The assassination failed.

So, the Order evolved.

No more ghosts. No more rebels.

Now, the city itself was the prison.

Then—every screen in the city flickered. All at once.

Billboards. Phones. Neon signs.

The noise of the world dropped to a hush— And the Architect's voice filled the vacuum.

"This ends tonight."

The hitman froze.

Muscles tight. Breath held. The feed shifted.

Her face.

Her real name.

Then—footage.

Clipped. Warped. Weaponized.

Her family's execution. The failed resistance. Her childhood in flames.

Private pain—now public spectacle.

Fabricated charges scrolled beneath.

TERRORIST. TRAITOR. TARGET.

Then bold, unmistakable letters:

PUBLIC ENEMY NUMBER ONE.

And a bounty.

Enough to turn strangers into killers. Enough to turn friends into monsters.

This wasn't execution. It was eradication.

The Architect returned.

"Turn yourself in." "Or watch her burn."

Then—A countdown.

4:00:00

Every face around them became a risk. Every eye a camera.

Every silence a threat. Not a city.

A weapon.

And now?

Every soul within it had a reason to sell them out.

Money. Revenge. Fear.

Survival.

She stared at the screens.

At her past—hijacked, corrupted.

Her breath caught— Only for a second.

He stepped closer.

His voice low. Controlled. But inside?

Fire.

"They think we're cornered."

She looked up.

Steady. Focused. Unafraid. "Then let's make them regret it." They didn't speak again.

No more hiding. No more running.

This wasn't their war anymore. It was their judgment.

And tonight?

The city would choose.

Or burn.

Chater 33 – Infiltrating the Heart of the Order

The city turned against them.

Her face lit up every screen, her name whispered like both curse and currency.

Wanted.

Hunted.

The Order thought they'd won. They were wrong.

This wasn't desperation. It was execution.

And the hitman?

He wasn't playing their game anymore. He was ending it.

The Architect was waiting.

High above sealed in the heart of the beast.

A skyscraper built of steel, glass, and God-complex. Disguised as progress.

Wired like a war machine.

Biometric locks. Drone patrols.

Elite enforcers stationed like blood cells in a living organism.

They built it to keep armies out. But they weren't ready for ghosts.

They entered from below.

Access tunnels beneath the city—forgotten arteries pulsing with dust and memory.

No alarms.

No lights.

Only silence.

Only death.

The first guards never saw it coming. One breath. One bullet. Gone.

She moved behind him—fluid and focused.

A drone buzzed overhead—Her silenced shot shattered its eye. Sparks flickered like fireflies.

They were inside.

Every floor was war. Turrets. Laser webs.

Men trained to kill without blinking. But it wasn't enough.

He moved like vengeance sculpted into flesh. Precise. Silent. Unstoppable.

She followed—surgical and ruthless.

Not just surviving—cutting through the lie.

This wasn't chaos. It was math.

Cold.

Perfect.

And still—each step took her closer to the place she feared most.

This building.

This machine.

The place that swallowed her family, her cause, her name. But now?

Now she had a new name.

Hunter.

She wasn't here to die.

She was here to make sure no one else had to live like this.

Not again.

The elevator hissed open. The top floor.

Command level.

No alarms now. They were expected.

The doors parted like the jaws of a monster. Inside—Armoured enforcers. Weapons raised.

A half-circle of polished death.

And beyond them, on a raised dais: The Architect.

Not a face.

A presence.

Calm. Cold. Almost curious. "You really think you've won?"

The hitman chambered his last round. The sound was final.

She turned to him. Eyes clear.

Jaw set.

A single nod.

Not fear.

Choice.

"Let's finish this."

Chapter 34 – The Architect's Final Truth

The doors opened with a whisper. No guards.

No alarms.

No bullets.

Just him.

The Architect.

Seated in a glass-walled sanctum at the top of the world. The burning city reflected below his feet like a grave made of light.

Calm.

Waiting.

As if this—all of it—was always the plan.

Weapons raised. Breaths sharp.

No hesitation left.

No questions... or so they thought.

The hitman stepped forward. Gun levelled.

"You lose."

The Architect didn't flinch. "Do I?"

He gestured toward the surrounding screens— Still flickering.

Still alive.

The Order's networks pulsed quietly in the background.

"Pull the trigger," he said. "Watch nothing change."

The hitman's grip tightened— But the bullet didn't come.

Not yet.

"What's your play?" the woman asked. Her voice didn't shake.

It sliced.

"You murdered my family. You built this machine."

The Architect turned to her. Not with guilt.

With curiosity.

"No," he said, softly. "We did."

He stood.

No threat in the motion. No fear either.

"There is no single Architect," he said. "Only the chair. The function. The cycle."

"Kill me," he offered.

"And another takes my place. You misunderstand... the system doesn't die. It evolves."

The hitman said nothing.

But his stance shifted—barely. And the Architect saw it.

"Why do you think we fought you so hard?" "It wasn't resistance. It was refinement."

"You weren't built to destroy the Order." A pause.

A truth.

A blade.

"You were built to lead it."

The room shifted. Not physically.

But in meaning.

Suddenly the blood. The betrayals. The pain— It wasn't punishment.

It was programming. Preparation.

She stepped back a pace. Not out of fear.

She watched him now. Carefully.

The way his jaw clenched.

The way the silence stretched taut in his chest.

"It was never about control," the Architect continued. "It was about preparing you for power."

"You already lead. You already command. You already kill with purpose."

He sat back down. At peace.

"Kill me, and the wheel keeps turning." "But sit in my place?"

"You break the wheel." The gun trembled.

His thoughts—sharper than the muzzle. Was any of it his?

The vengeance. The rebellion.

The rage.

Or had they written this ending before he ever picked up a weapon?

She didn't move. Didn't speak.

She just watched.

Not afraid of what he'd do.

But afraid of what he might become. This wasn't just the end of the Order. It was the end of him.

The barrel pointed. The trigger waited.

One bullet could erase the past.

But what would rise from the ashes?

Chapter 35 – The Temptation of Power

The hitman didn't lower his gun. But he didn't fire.

The Architect sat motionless. Calm.

Certain.

Watching.

Hesitation.

That was all he needed.

She saw it.

His stance—still taut.

His grip—still white-knuckled. But beneath the rage?

Doubt.

And doubt... was the first chain.

"Think about it," the Architect said.

His voice smooth, measured. A serpent's whisper. "The Order will never die. But under you..." He leaned forward, eyes gleaming.

"You could reshape it."

"End the chaos. Control the violence." "Decide who lives. Who rules. Who survives."

His smirk returned.

"You think you're burning the system?" "You're just giving it to the next monster."

"Might as well be a monster with a conscience."

The hitman's breath slowed. Finger twitching over the trigger.

This was it.

The moment.

Pull the trigger—and end it.

But then what?

The machine keeps turning.

Someone else rises. Maybe worse.

Or maybe... Maybe it should be him. She moved.

Close now. Too close.

Her voice wasn't sharp anymore. It was frayed. Real.

"This is what they made you for." "Not to kill. Not to follow."

"To replace them."

Her eyes locked on his.

For the first time— She looked afraid.

Not of what he'd do.

Afraid of what he'd become.

The Architect chuckled.

"Why are you listening to her?"

"She doesn't understand what you are." He tilted his head—almost gentle.

"I do."

And the hitman saw it.

A world that feared him. Obeyed him.

A world shaped by his hand.

No more chains. No more targets.

He gives the orders now.

He would be the fire they worshipped. The ghost they feared.

Not hunted. Remembered.

She shook her head.

Her voice cracked—but didn't break.

"If you do this..."

"You're not saving anyone." "You're just becoming him."

Silence.

He didn't speak. Because deep inside— He knew she was right.

But another voice—The one made of pain and silence and blood—whispered: And what if that's the only way to win?

The Architect waited. Still. Patient.

Because this?

This was the moment they had built him for.

She waited too.

No weapon. No threat. Just hope.

Fractured. Fading.

And the hitman?

He didn't look at either of them.

He looked inward. At the line.

Thin. Final.

One step across—And he becomes the very thing he swore to destroy.

Because this was never about vengeance.

Or rebellion.

Or even survival.

This was about choice.

And now?

He had one.

Chapter 36 - The Final Test

The hitman stood between two futures.

The Architect—seated, calm, patient.

The woman—silent, watching, already bracing for loss.

This wasn't a decision. It was a reckoning.

The final one.

"You're still unsure," the Architect said. A tilt of the head. Clinical. Measuring. "That's natural."

A slow smile followed. Predatory. Certain. "Let me make it easier."

He nodded.

A door hissed open. Inside—A single metal chair. Steel. Restrained. Waiting. A throne or a tomb.

"Sit," the Architect said.

"Take your place. Rewrite history." A beat.

"Or put her in the chair— and walk away as you were." "Nothing."

Her breath caught.

She understood instantly. This wasn't survival.

It was severance.

Take the seat— and she dies.

The last part of him that still felt human. Erased.

He saw the paths before him:

Power. Command.

A world that obeyed.

No more chains. No more orders. No more fear.

Just control.

But the cost?

Her.

The Architect's voice softened—the kind of softness that breaks bones.

"You can't have both."

"We don't love. We don't attach." "We command."

She stepped forward. Unarmed.

Unflinching.

Unafraid.

"If you do this…"

"You don't just lose me." "You lose yourself."

Her voice was steel wrapped in sorrow. "Who are you without them?"

He said nothing.

His fingers hovered over his weapon. Memories surged.

Missions.

Targets.

Blood.

Silence.

All of it had brought him here. And yet—She was the only thing that had ever felt real.

The Architect leaned back. Smiling.

"Make your choice."

She didn't look away. Neither did he.

And then—he took one breath. A single breath.

Not of fear. Not of fury.

Of clarity.

The breath of a man choosing what kind of ghost he wanted to be.

Chapter 37 - Rejecting the Order

The hitman closed his eyes. Just for a second.

The Architect's voice still echoed—smooth, certain, laced with poison.

Across the room, she stood silent. Watching.

Knowing.

This was the moment that would decide everything. And then—He understood.

There had never been a choice. Because he had never been theirs.

His weapon moved before the next word could fall. One shot.

Clean. Final.

The Architect's head snapped back— and the body slumped in the chair, smirk still etched on a now-empty face.

But now?

It was over. The room froze.

Guards stiffened. No orders.

No hierarchy. Only silence. Only confusion.

And that hesitation? It was enough.

Gunfire erupted.

Blood painted power's walls.

Back-to-back, they moved as one. Swift. Precise. Final.

Not rebels.

Not survivors.

Executioners of an era.

And then—The system began to die. Monitors flickered.

Files shredded themselves. Firewalls collapsed.

Sirens wailed a death cry. This wasn't a design.

It was a purge.

Not planned by the Architect. But triggered by his death.

The Order had built itself without a conscience. Now it crumbled without one.

The hitman didn't think of the past. Not the missions.

Not the mentors. Not the lies.

He had been a weapon. Now he was a man.

And he chose his own target.

She watched him— not as a machine. Not as a tool.

But as himself.

He hadn't chosen the throne. He hadn't chosen control.

He chose freedom.

And he chose her. The facility burned.

The machine imploded. But this wasn't the end. Not yet.

Not until the last shadow vanished.

Not until the world saw what had lived in its walls.

He paused over the Architect's body. Just one breath.

Then turned to her. "We finish this."

And together—they disappeared into the fire. Not to die.

But to make sure no one else would ever be built in their image again.

Chapter 38 - Erasing the Order

Behind them, the tower fell.

Stone and steel swallowed in fire. But killing a man wasn't victory. Because the Order wasn't a man. It was a machine.

And machines don't die until you kill their memory.

She pulled out the stolen data drive. Small. Plain.

But inside?

Everything.

Names. Ledgers. Black sites. Programs.

The backbone.

Coordinates flickered on the cracked screen. A final thread.

A place the Order never thought they'd find.

A bunker—buried beneath the city's spine. Old world.

Cold war.

Steel-forged to survive anything. Including truth.

No map listed it.

No network pinged it. But they found it.

Because they had to.

They moved through concrete arteries.

Ghosts under a city that had no idea it was finally free. The last guards fell in silence.

There was no defiance. No backup.

Just fear.

The mainframe waited.

Rows of servers glowing with soft, pulsing light. Alive. A god at rest.

She stepped forward. Inserted the drive.

Lines of code surged to life. The virus launched.

28%. 53%. 78%. 91%...

Almost done.

Almost free.

A voice echoed—smooth, familiar, pre-recorded. "You think you've won?"

The Architect's ghost.

"The Order isn't a person. It's an idea." "Someone will rebuild. They always do." She didn't flinch.

She didn't argue.

She just pressed [EXECUTE]. The servers stuttered.

Then glowed red.

Data unravelled.

History deleted itself, line by line.

Proof. Legacy. Power.

Gone.

One final guard stood in the corner. Unarmed.

Frozen.

He waited—hoping for mercy. The hitman didn't blink.

One shot.

Silent.

Final.

The alarms screamed. The bunker groaned. Self-destruct online.

They ran—through smoke, through steel, through collapsing corridors.

And behind them?

An empire vanished.

The city above exhaled.

For the first time in decades, no one watched.

No screens.

No checkpoints.

No voice in the walls. Just silence.

And sky.

She stood beside him. Whole.

Breathing.

Alive.

He turned to her. "It's over."

She nodded. But in her eyes? Not relief.

Not triumph. Something quieter. Something harder.

"What do you do when the war is won?"

Chapter 39 - The Ghosts That Never Die

The city looked different now.

Quieter. Lighter.

Like something had been lifted—but not removed.

The Order was gone. But peace?

Peace was just a story people told themselves in the dark.

No victory speech. No broadcast.

No one cheered.

Ghosts don't get parades. They get silence.

They vanished.

Like they'd never existed at all.

For the first time, there was no target. No mission.

No war.

She sat beside him. "What now?" she asked. He didn't answer.

Because he didn't know.

He had never lived outside the hunt.

Weeks passed.

A hideout in the trees. Cold wind.

Distant quiet.

Then—A flicker on the terminal.

An encryption key long buried came alive. A message.

No name.

No sender.

Just one line: You did well. We'll be watching.

His pulse didn't race. It stopped.

He ran the trace. Too clean.

Too elegant.

Not a survivor. Not a mistake.

A contingency.

She leaned in, read the words. Then looked at him.

"Tell me this doesn't mean what I think it means."

He didn't respond. He didn't have to.

The Architect wasn't the end. There was no end.

The Order wasn't a man. Not a council.

It was an idea.

And ideas don't die. They replicate.

He hadn't destroyed it.

He'd triggered the next phase.

Maybe he wasn't the solution.

Maybe he was just proof the system worked.

She whispered, voice steady— but hollowed out.

"What do we do?"

He stared at the screen. At the ghost in the wires.

He exhaled. Then—finally—smiled.

"We make sure they never get the chance." He thought the war was over.

He was wrong.

Some systems don't fall. They adapt.

And now?

He was the only one who truly understood what they were. Not a rebel.

Not a killer. A firewall.

One figure on a rooftop, watching a city that never really belonged to itself.

Waiting.

Guarding.

Because some wars don't end. And he wasn't done yet.

The End

Printed in Dunstable, United Kingdom